WHY THE CHIMES RANG

WHY
THE CHIMES
RANG

By

RAYMOND
MACDONALD
ALDEN

Decorated by
MAYO BUNKER

INDIANAPOLIS
THE BOBBS-MERRILL COMPANY
PUBLISHERS

WHY THE CHIMES RANG

HERE was once, in a far-away country where few people have ever traveled, a wonderful church. It stood on a high hill in the midst

 of a great city; and every Sunday, as well as on sacred days like Christmas, thousands of people climbed the hill to its great archways, looking like lines of ants all moving in the same direction.

When you came to the building itself, you found stone columns and dark passages, and a grand entrance leading to the main room of the church. This room was so long that one standing at the doorway could scarcely see to the other end, where the choir stood by the marble altar. In the farthest corner was the organ; and this organ was so loud, that sometimes when it played, the people for miles around would close their shutters and prepare for a great thunderstorm. Alto-

gether, no such church as this was ever seen before, especially when it was lighted up for some festival, and crowded with people, young and old. But the strangest thing about the whole building was the wonderful chime of bells.

At one corner of the church was a great gray tower, with ivy growing over it as far up as one could see. I say as far as one could see,

because the tower was quite great
enough to fit the great church,
and it rose so far into the sky that
it was only in very fair weather
that any one claimed to be able to
see the top.   Even then one could
not be certain that it was in sight.
Up, and up, and up climbed the
stones and the ivy; and, as the
men who built the church had

been dead for hundreds of years, every one had forgotten how high the tower was supposed to be.

Now all the people knew that at the top of the tower was a chime of Christmas bells. They had hung there ever since the church had been built, and were the most beautiful bells in the world. Some

thought it was because a great
musician had cast them and
arranged them in their place;
others said it was because of the
great height, which reached up
where the air was clearest and
purest: however that might be,
no one who had ever heard the
chimes denied that they were the

sweetest in the world. Some described them as sounding

like angels far up
in the sky; others,
as sounding like
strange winds sing-
ing through the
trees.

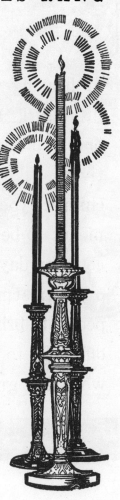

But the fact was
that no one had
heard them for
years and years.
There was an old
man living not far
from the church,
who said that his
mother had spoken

of hearing them when she was a
little girl, and he was the only
one who was sure of as much as
that. They were Christmas
chimes, you see, and were not
meant to be played by men or on
common days. It was the custom
on Christmas Eve for all the
people to bring to the church their
offerings to the Christ-child; and
when the greatest and best offer-

ing was laid on the altar, there used to come sounding through the music of the choir the Christmas chimes far up in the tower. Some said that the wind rang them, and others that they were so high that the angels could set them swinging. But for many long years they had never been heard. It was said that people had been growing less careful of

their gifts for the Christ-child, and that no offering was brought, great enough to deserve the music of the chimes.

Every Christmas Eve the rich people

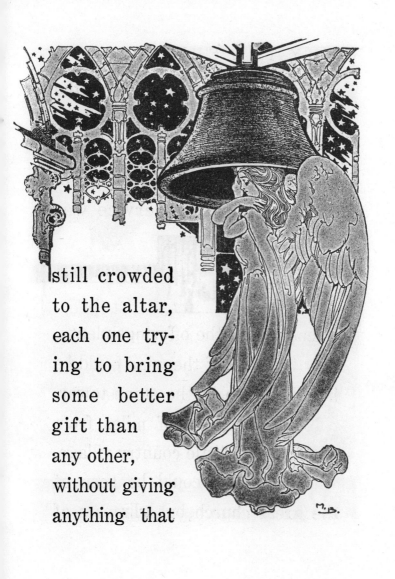

still crowded
to the altar,
each one try-
ing to bring
some better
gift than
any other,
without giving
anything that

he wanted for himself, and the church was crowded with those who thought that perhaps the wonderful bells might be heard again. But although the service was

splendid, and the offerings plenty, only the roar of the wind could be heard, far up in the stone tower.

Now, a number of miles from the city, in a little country village, where nothing could be seen of the great church but glimpses of the tower when the weather was fine, lived a boy named Pedro, and his little brother. They knew very little about the Christmas chimes, but they had heard of the

service in the church on Christmas Eve, and had a secret plan, which they had often talked over when by themselves, to go to see the beautiful celebration.

"Nobody can guess, Little Brother," Pedro would say, "all

WHY THE CHIMES RANG

the fine things there are to see and hear;

and I have even

heard it said that the Christ-child sometimes comes down to bless the service. What if we could see Him?

The day before Christmas was bitterly cold, with a few lonely snowflakes flying in the air, and a hard white crust on the ground. Sure enough, Pedro and Little Brother were able to slip quietly away early in the after-

noon; and although the walking
was hard in the frosty air, before
nightfall they had trudged so far,
hand in   hand, that they
saw the   lights of the big
city just   ahead of them.
Indeed, they

were about to enter one of the great gates in the wall that surrounded it, when they saw something dark on the snow near their path, and stepped aside to look at it.

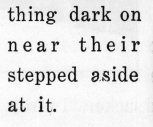

It was a poor woman, who had fallen just out-side the city, too sick and tired to get in where she  might have found shelter. The soft snow made of a drift a sort of pillow for her, and she would soon be so sound asleep, in the wintry air, that no one could ever waken her again. All this Pedro saw in a moment, and he knelt down beside her and tried to rouse her, even tugging at her arm a little, as

though he would have tried to carry her away. He turned her face toward him, so that he could rub some of the snow on it, and when he had looked at her silently a moment he stood up again, and said:

"It's no use, Little Brother. You will have to go on alone."

"Alone?" cried Little Brother. "And you not see the Christmas festival?"

"No," said Pedro, and he could not keep back a bit of a choking sound in his throat. "See this poor woman. Her face looks like the Madonna in the chapel window, and she will freeze to death if nobody cares for her. Every one has gone to the church

now, but when you come back you can bring some one to help her. I will rub her to keep her from freezing, and perhaps get her to eat the bun that is left in my pocket."

"But I can not bear to leave you, and go on alone," said Little Brother.

"Both of us need not miss the service," said Pedro, "and it had better be I than you. You can

easily find your way to the church; and you must see and hear everything twice, Little Brother—once for you and once for me. I am sure the Christ-child must know how I should love to come with you and worship Him; and oh! if you get a chance, Little Brother, to slip up to the altar without getting in any one's way, take this little silver piece of mine, and lay it down for my offer-

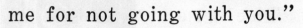

ing, when no one is
looking. Do not for-
get where you have
left me, and forgive
me for not going with you."

In this way he hurried Little
Brother off to the city, and
winked hard to keep back the
tears, as he heard the crunching
footsteps sounding farther and
farther away in the twilight. It

was pretty hard to
lose the music and
splendor of the
Christmas celebra-

tion that he had been planning for so long, and spend the time instead in that lonely place in the snow.

The great church was a wonderful place that night. Every one said that it had never looked so bright and beautiful before. When the organ played and the thousands of people sang, the walls shook with the sound, and little Pedro, away outside the city wall, felt the earth tremble around him.

At the close of the service came the procession with the offerings

to be laid on the altar. Rich men and great men marched proudly up to lay down their gifts to the Christ-child. Some brought wonderful jewels, some baskets of gold so heavy that they could scarcely carry them down the aisle. A great writer laid down a book that he had been making

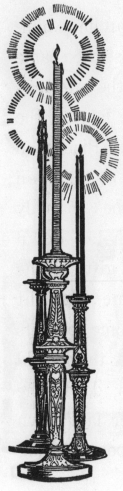

for years and years.
And last of all
walked the king of
the country, hoping
with all the rest to
win for himself the
chime of the Christ-
mas bells. There
went a great mur-
mur through the
church, as the people
saw the king take
from his head the
royal crown, all
set with precious

stones, and lay it gleaming on the altar, as his offering to the holy Child. "Surely," every one said, "we shall hear the bells now, for nothing like this has ever happened before."

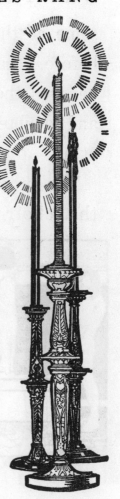

But still only the cold old wind was heard in the tower, and the people shook their heads; and some of them said, as they had before, that they never really believed the story of the chimes, and doubted if they ever rang at all.

The procession was over, and the choir began the closing hymn. Suddenly the organist stopped playing as though

 he had been shot, and every one looked at the old minister, who was standing by the altar, holding up his hand for silence. Not a sound could be heard from any one in the church, but as all the people strained their ears to listen, there came softly, but distinctly, swinging through the air, the sound of the chimes in the tower. So far away, and

yet so clear the music seemed—so much sweeter were the notes than any-thing that had been heard before, rising and falling away up there in the sky, that the people in

the church sat for a moment as still as though something held each of them by the shoulders. Then they all stood up together and stared straight at the altar, to see what great gift had

awakened the long-silent bells.

But all that the nearest of them saw was the childish figure of Little Brother, who had crept softly down the aisle when no one was look-ing, and had laid Pedro's little piece of silver on the altar.